To

YASMIN

MOUSE AND ELEPHANT
Written by An Vrombaut
Illustrated by An Vrombaut
British Library Cataloguing in Publication Data
A catalogue record of this book is available from the British Library
ISBN 0 340 74426 X (HB)
ISBN 0 340 74427 8 (PB)
Text copyright © An Vrombaut 2000
Illustrations copyright © An Vrombaut 2000

The right of An Vrombaut to be identified as author
of the text of this work, and of An Vrombaut to be
identified as the illustrator of this work
has been asserted by her in accordance with the
Copyright, Design and Patents Act 1988

First edition published 2000
10 9 8 7 6 5 4 3 2 1

Published by Hodder Children's Books,
a division of Hodder Headline,
338 Euston Road, London NW1 3BH

Printed in Hong Kong

Mouse and Elephant

An Vrombaut

Hodder Children's Books

A division of Hodder Headline

Mouse wants to
play a game with Elephant.

What can they play?
Can they . . .

. . . play
basketball?

Elephant
likes
basketball.

But Mouse
does not!

Can they . . .

. . . play football?

Mouse likes football.
But Elephant
does not!

Can they . . .

Elephant likes bouncing.
But Mouse does not!

What can they play?
Can they . . .

. . . walk on the tightrope?
Mouse can (just about).
But Elephant cannot!

Elephant does not
like ballooning.

Mouse does not feel like flying a kite.

Elephant really
does not
feel like
parachute
jumping!

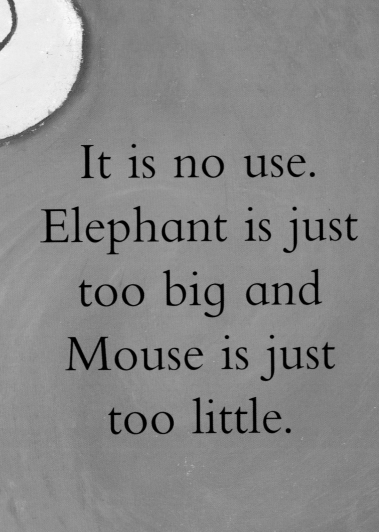

It is no use.
Elephant is just
too big and
Mouse is just
too little.

Then Elephant has an idea!

Hammer, hammer!
Bang, crash, bang, ouch!

Elephant has made . . .

. . . a tricycle
that is just right . . .

. . .a mouse-and-elephant-tricycle

. . .made for two!